MY BEST FRIEND TURNED ME INTO THE PERFECT WOMAN

Gay Sissy Feminization Story

Lumia Longwood

Copyright © 2025 Lumia Longwood

All rights reserved

The characters and events portrayed in this book are fictitious. Any similarity to real persons, living or dead, is coincidental and not intended by the author.

No part of this book may be reproduced, or stored in a retrieval system, or transmitted in any form or by any means, electronic, mechanical, photocopying, recording, or otherwise, without express written permission of the publisher.

ISBN: 9798293171897
Imprint: Independently published

1st edition

CONTENTS

Title Page
Copyright
Chapter 1   1
Chapter 2   9
Chapter 3   17
Chapter 4   22
Chapter 5   30
Chapter 6   39
Chapter 7   44
Chapter 8   51
Chapter 9   60
Epilogue   71
More by Lumia   79
About the Author   81

CHAPTER 1

Oh, fuck. I hated this. Not because of Amelia, but because she always wanted to talk about him at these godforsaken mornings, when all I craved was a quiet moment over coffee and croissants.

The sun hadn't even graced us with its presence yet, but here we were, in this dimly lit corner of our usual café, her eyes already sparkling with that annoying glee she reserved only for talking about *him.*

It could easily get annoying sometimes.

"August," Amelia began, stirring her cappuccino with meticulous slowness. I knew what was coming next. "Guess who's back from his trip?"

I sighed internally, taking a sip of my black coffee to stall my response. The bitter liquid scalded my tongue, mirroring the burn of jealousy that had become all too familiar. I didn't want to have that feeling, but couldn't stop it. "Oh, let me guess," I drawled. "The big, bad lumberjack."

She giggled, her eyes twinkling with amusement and something else I refused to acknowledge. "You're just jealous because he can grow a real beard."

I rolled my eyes, running a hand over the smooth skin of my chin. "Yeah, well, not all of us are blessed with the ability to look like a yeti." My fingers itched to trace the faint stubble on my jaw, but I resisted, not wanting her to see how much her words affected me.

This was such a drag.

Amelia leaned in, her eyes sparkling again. "He sent me pictures from his trip, August. You should've seen him, standing there in the middle of the forest, his shirt off—"

Yeah, I didn't need to picture that in my mind. I was already too horny.

"Okay, okay," I interrupted, holding up my hands in surrender. My heart pounded in my chest, and I could feel the heat creeping up my neck. "I get it. He's a rugged, muscular god among men." I emphasized the words, hoping to sound sarcastic rather than envious.

She laughed, sitting back in her chair. "He really is."

I took another sip of my coffee, trying to focus on anything but the image of him burning itself into my mind. "So," I said, changing the subject. "What did you two get up to last night?" My tone was casual, but I felt anything but.

Amelia's eyes lit up again, and she began to recount their evening, oblivious to the storm of emotions brewing inside me.

I listened, offering appropriate responses at the right times, but my mind was elsewhere. It was with him—with his rough hands, his deep voice, his laugh that rumbled like thunder.

With the way he looked at Amelia like she was the most precious thing in the world.

My fingers tapped nervously against the side of my mug as I zoned out, lost in my own thoughts. I had known for a long time now that my feelings for her boyfriend were more than just friendly admiration.

But I pushed them down, buried them under layers of denial and self-loathing. I was straight, wasn't I? At least, I thought I was.

"August?" Amelia's voice pulled me back to reality. "Are you even listening to me?"

I blinked, focusing on her face. "Sorry," I muttered. "Just... tired."

She raised an eyebrow but let it go. "Well, if you're that tired, why don't we call it a night early? We can catch up another time."

I was already 18.

God, where did the time go? It felt like just yesterday I was celebrating my seventeenth birthday, and now here I was, a college student with no idea what I wanted in life.

Well, that wasn't entirely true. I knew what I wanted—who I wanted—but it was an impossible fantasy, a pipe dream that would never come true.

I took another sip of my coffee, letting the bitter liquid distract me from my thoughts. My mind raced, memories and desires jumbling together into one big mess.

Why did Amelia have to bring him up again? I knew she meant well, but every time she talked about her boyfriend, it felt like a dagger twisting in my heart. I couldn't help but compare myself to him—his strength, his confidence, the way he took charge of everything and everyone around him.

And then there was me. Eighteen years old, a virgin, and never even been on a proper date. Hell, I had never even kissed anyone before. What did I have to offer?

I sighed internally, tracing patterns on the table with my fingers. My gaze drifted to my reflection in the window, and for a moment, I didn't recognize myself. My hair was longer than most guys'—it reached just below my shoulders now—and I had started experimenting with makeup when no one was looking.

It all started as a joke, really. A dare from Amelia to try on some of her lipstick. But then I saw the way it made me look—that hint of pink adding something soft and almost feminine to my face—and I couldn't stop. It was addictive.

I liked the way it felt, the way it transformed me into someone else. Someone confident, brave, fearless. Someone who could have what they wanted.

But why did that person have to be a girl?

I shook my head, dispelling the thoughts. It didn't matter, not really. I was straight, wasn't I? Sure, I liked dressing up as a girl sometimes, but that was just... a thing I did. A way to escape from reality for a little while.

It didn't change who I was inside. Or what I wanted.

And what I wanted was him.

But how could I ever tell Amelia that? How could I confess my feelings for her boyfriend without ruining everything between us? She was my best friend. Losing her would be devastating.

Not to mention the fact that he was straight too. Even if I found the courage to admit my feelings, there was no guarantee he'd feel the same way. Hell, he probably wouldn't even understand what I was talking about.

I sighed again, rubbing my temples with my fingertips. This was all so fucked up. Why did life have to be so complicated?

I wanted things to go back to normal—to before Amelia started dating him, before I realized the extent of my feelings for her boyfriend, before I even knew what it meant to want someone like this.

But then again, maybe 'normal' wasn't what I really wanted.

Maybe I wanted something else entirely, something scary and uncertain and completely out of my comfort zone. Maybe I wanted to take a chance, to put myself out there and see where things went.

The thought sent a shiver down my spine, both thrilling and terrifying at the same time. Could I do it? Could I actually tell Amelia how I felt?

Or would it be better to keep everything buried deep inside, like I had been doing for so long now?

I didn't know the answer. But I knew that I couldn't keep living in this limbo forever. Eventually, I was going to have to make a choice, one way or another.

My eyes flicked back to the window, my reflection staring back at me with an intensity I hadn't noticed before. I saw the way my gaze lingered on my lips, now stained a soft pink from Amelia's lipstick earlier today.

I couldn't help but wonder what it would be like to have his cock in my mouth.

Not just any cock—his. Big, thick, and throbbing with too much lust. Just thinking about it sent shivers down my spine and made me squirm uncomfortably in my seat.

God, I was such a fucking pervert. What kind of straight guy thought about sucking another man's dick?

But here I was, fantasizing about exactly that, and I had no hope of stopping it.

I took another sip of coffee, trying to distract myself from the thoughts swirling around in my head like a storm. It didn't work. Instead, all it did was make me think about how he would taste, dark and bitter like coffee, maybe, with a hint of saltiness that made me lick my lips involuntarily.

Fuck, fuck, fuck. I needed to stop this. Now.

I closed my eyes, taking a deep breath in an attempt to calm myself down. It didn't help. All it did was bring back memories of the last time I saw him, with his strong arms flexing as he chopped wood outside their house, sweat glistening on his tanned skin, the way his jeans hugged his bulge perfectly.

And then there was that one moment when he caught me staring at him. His lips quirked into a half-smile, and he winked at me before turning back to his work.

Had he known? Did he realize what I wanted from him?

The thought made my heart pound even faster, sending heat rushing through my veins. I could feel myself getting hard, the front of my jeans tenting slightly as I shifted in my seat again.

God, I needed to get out of here before Amelia noticed something was wrong. She'd kill me if she found out about these thoughts—these desires—and I didn't blame her. It was fucked up, and I knew it.

But still... I couldn't stop myself from thinking about him. About what he would feel like in my mouth, about how his hands would grip my hair as he fucked my face, about the sounds he'd make when he fed me his hot cum.

I swallowed hard, trying to push the thoughts away once more. This was dangerous territory, and I needed to steer clear of it if I didn't want to ruin everything between Amelia and me.

But then again, who was I kidding? Everything was already ruined because of my fucked-up feelings for her boyfriend.

I stood up abruptly, grabbing my coat and bag. "Hey, I gotta go," I said, barely looking at Amelia as I rushed past her. "See you later, okay?"

I tried to make a run for it, but Amelia wasn't having any of that. She reached out and grabbed my wrist before I could escape, her fingers digging into my skin with surprising strength.

"Hey, where do you think you're going?" she asked, her voice as sharp as a whip. "I'm not done talking to you yet."

I sighed again, knowing there was no use arguing with her when she got like this. I reluctantly sat back down in my chair, trying my best to appear casual even though every nerve ending in my body felt like it was on fire.

"Fine," I muttered. "But can we make this quick? I've got shit to do."

Amelia raised an eyebrow at me but didn't say anything else

about my sudden urge to leave. Instead, she leaned back in her chair and crossed her legs, a smirk playing on her lips.

"So, you asked before about last night and I have to say it was interesting... very interesting, to say the least," she said, drawing out the words for emphasis.

I rolled my eyes, already dreading where this conversation was going. "Please, spare me the details. I don't want to know how many times you two fucked like rabbits."

She laughed, completely unfazed. "Oh, come on, August. Don't be such a prude. You can handle it."

I doubted that very much, but before I could say anything else, she continued.

"It was fucking incredible, okay? He was so... *him.*" She bit her lip, her eyes glazing over as if lost in some distant memory. "He took me from behind, hard and fast, just the way I like it."

My heart pounded in my chest, and I felt my face grow hot with embarrassment, and that same thing I didn't want to admit was there too.

I shifted uncomfortably in my seat, trying to hide the fact that her words were having a very unwelcome effect on me.

Amelia didn't seem to notice or care. She just kept going, her voice getting huskier with each word. "I could feel him so deep inside of me, filling me up completely. God, it was amazing."

She paused for a moment, her tongue darting out to lick her lips. I watched the movement, unable to look away, and felt my cock twitch in response.

"He fucked me so hard that I couldn't even walk straight this morning," she continued, laughing softly. "I'm still sore, but it's a good kind of soreness. You know what I mean?"

No, no, I did not want to know anything about her 'good' soreness. But before I could tell her to stop talking about it, she went on.

"I can show you," she whispered, her breath hot against my ear. "If you want."

The fuck?

I froze, my body tense. What was she suggesting? Did she really think that...?

Before I could even finish the thought, Amelia pulled away from me, grinning like a cat who had just caught its prey.

"Just kidding," she said, laughing at the expression on my face. "You should've seen your face, though. Priceless."

I sat there in stunned silence for a moment, trying to process what had just happened. Had she really just offered...?

No. No way. There was no fucking way that Amelia would ever—

"August?" Amelia's voice interrupted my thoughts, her tone suddenly serious again. "Are you okay? You look pale."

I blinked, finally managing to find my voice. "Yeah," I said hoarsely. "I'm fine. Just... need some air, I think."

Without waiting for her response, I stood up and made a beeline for the door, leaving my half-finished coffee behind. I needed to get out of here, and fast.

This was too much. Too fucking much. My best friend talking about her boyfriend's dick like that, offering... things... to me...

I shuddered at the thought, pushing open the café door and stepping outside into the cool morning air. It wasn't until then that I realized my hands were shaking and my heart was still pounding wildly in my chest.

What the fuck had just happened?

CHAPTER 2

My mind was still spinning from our conversation at the café as I walked down the familiar street towards Amelia's house. The sun beat down on me, its rays seemingly amplified through the clear blue sky above, and sweat trickled down my back despite the early hour.

But it wasn't just the heat that made me feel so flushed. No, it was the image of her boyfriend—her rugged, muscular, incredibly virile boyfriend—that kept playing over and over in my mind like a fucked-up slideshow I couldn't shut off.

I tried to push away the thoughts as I turned the corner onto their street, but they clung to me like a second skin. I could practically feel his hands on me, calloused from years of hard work and rough because he didn't know how to be gentle. I imagined them gripping my hips tightly, pulling me against him as he...

Fuck.

I shook my head, trying to clear it, but it was no use. The more I tried not to think about him, the more intense the thoughts became.

And then I saw him.

He was out in front of Amelia's house, shirtless and sweaty

as he chopped wood with precise, powerful strokes. His muscles flexed with each swing of the ax, his tattoos shifting and twisting like they had lives of their own.

God, he was a fucking god among men. *A real man.* Not some scrawny college kid like me who spent more time experimenting with makeup than actually doing anything useful.

I stopped walking, unable to tear my eyes away from the sight before me. I told myself that it was just because I hadn't seen him in a while—that anyone would appreciate such an impressive display of masculinity—but deep down, I knew the truth.

It was more than that. So much more.

He paused for a moment, wiping the sweat off his forehead with the back of his hand before taking another swing at the log in front of him. I watched as the ax sliced through it easily, splitting it into two neat pieces that fell to the ground with a soft thud.

I didn't even know why he was chopping wood. Maybe he just liked doing it. He certainly didn't need to.

And fuck, even his forearms were sexy. Veined and corded with muscle, they flexed in a way that made me want to trace the lines with my tongue.

I swallowed hard, trying to ignore the growing ache between my legs. This was wrong, so unbelievably fucking wrong. I shouldn't be thinking about him like this—especially not here, right out in the open where anyone could see me—but I couldn't help it.

There was something about him that called to me on a primal level, something that made me want to surrender completely and let him take control of every inch of my body.

I shifted uncomfortably, trying to relieve some of the pressure building in my groin. It didn't work. All it did was draw more attention to the fact that I was getting hard just from watching him chop wood, for fuck's sake.

What was wrong with me?

But even as I asked myself the question, I knew the answer. There was nothing 'wrong' with me. Not really. I just... felt things differently than most guys did. That didn't make me broken or messed up; it just made me who I was.

And right now, that meant standing here like an idiot while I watched my best friend's boyfriend chopping wood and fantasized about him fucking me senseless.

I bit my lip, suppressing a moan as he bent over to pick up another log. His ass looked amazing in those faded jeans, firm and round and practically begging for me to grab it.

What would it feel like to have him inside of me? To have his thick cock stretching me open, stuffing me completely?

I imagined what it might be like, the way he'd grip my hips tightly, pulling me back against him as he drove into me again and again. I could almost feel the heat of his body pressed against mine, hear the sound of our skin slapping together in a rhythm that would make us both pant.

Fuck, fuck, fuck.

I closed my eyes for a moment, trying to regain some semblance of control over myself. I was thinking things that were too dangerous—borderline obsession—and I knew it. But try as I might, I couldn't stop the fantasies from playing out in my mind like some kind of filthy movie that only I could see.

Thankfully, only I could see it, I thought.

And then, just when I thought things couldn't possibly get any worse, he looked up and caught me staring at him.

Our eyes met for what felt like an eternity, and time seemed to slow down around us. He didn't say anything, and quite frankly, he didn't have to. The intensity in his gaze said it all: he knew exactly what I was thinking about, and he liked it.

My heart pounded in my chest as we stared at each other,

my breathing becoming more erratic. It was as though he was challenging me to say something and break the tension.

But then, just as suddenly as it had started, the moment passed. He broke eye contact and turned back to his work, leaving me standing there alone on the sidewalk, feeling like an idiot.

I took a deep breath, trying to calm myself down before I did something stupid, like walking over there and throwing myself at him, but it was no use. My body felt alive in a way it never had before, every nerve ending tingling.

I wanted this—no, I *needed* this. More than anything else in the world, I needed to feel him inside of me, fucking me hard enough to make me forget everything except for the pleasure coursing through my veins.

But how was I supposed to make that happen? He was Amelia's boyfriend, not mine. And even if he were single—and interested—there was no way someone like him would want anything to do with a pathetic little virgin like me.

I sighed, finally managing to force myself to continue walking towards my house.

I was still lost in my thoughts, trying to process what had just happened between us, if anything even happened at all, when I heard footsteps approaching from behind me. I turned around slowly, half-expecting to see some kind of divine intervention or maybe even a mirage caused by the intense heat.

But no, it was neither of those things. It was Amelia, sauntering towards me with that same playful smirk she always wore when she knew something I didn't.

Fuck. Me.

My face felt hot instantly, and I looked away from her gaze, suddenly unable to meet her eyes. She stopped in front of me, hands on her hips as she surveyed the scene before us: her boyfriend still chopping wood, sweat glistening on his tanned skin, muscles flexing with each swing.

"I see you've been enjoying the view," she said, raising an eyebrow at me.

I swallowed hard, my mouth dry all of a sudden. "W-what are you talking about?" I stammered, trying to play dumb even though we both knew it was useless.

She laughed, shaking her head. "Oh, come on, August. Don't give me that shit. You know exactly what I'm talking about." She gestured towards her boyfriend with a nod of her chin. "You were checking him out."

I felt my face grow even hotter if that was possible, and I knew I must be beet red at this point. But before I could say anything else in my defense—assuming there was one—I saw the corners of her mouth twitching like she was trying not to laugh.

"You're cute when you're flustered," she said, reaching out to ruffle my hair. "But don't worry, your secret is safe with me."

I let out a sigh, knowing that it wasn't just my 'secret' she knew about but also how much I'd been fantasizing about her boyfriend. The thought made my stomach twist, and I couldn't help but feel a pang of guilt.

But then again, maybe this was my chance to finally put an end to these feelings once and for all. Maybe if I spent some real time with him and saw that he wasn't as perfect as I imagined, my stupid crush would finally fade away.

Yeah, right, said a voice in the back of my mind. *You can't even look at him without getting hard, remember?*

I pushed the thought aside, determined to keep trying nonetheless. "Can we just... go inside?" I asked Amelia, avoiding her gaze. "It's hot out here."

She shrugged, turning towards the house. "Sure thing," she said over her shoulder. "But first, let me introduce you properly to Colton. He's been asking about you, actually."

My heart stuttered in my chest at the sound of his name, and

I felt my palms start to sweat as I followed her up the front path.

He'd been asking about me. Why? What had she told him about me?

Also, what did he want to know about me for? And why now, when all I wanted was to run away from this situation as fast as possible?

Amelia didn't give me time to dwell on those questions, though. She led me straight over to where Colton was still chopping wood, a sheen of sweat covering his bare chest and making the tattoos there seem even more vivid than usual.

He paused in mid-swing when he saw us approaching, his eyes meeting mine for just long enough to make my breath hitch before turning towards Amelia. "Hey babe," he said, flashing her one of those smiles that made her light up like a fucking Christmas tree.

"Hi honey," she replied, leaning in to kiss him briefly on the lips. She pulled away all too soon, though, and turned back towards me with an excited grin. "Colton, you remember my best friend August, right?"

I felt my face grow hot again as he looked at me, his expression inscrutable. But then, slowly, one corner of his mouth lifted in a smirk that made me stop breathing for an entire second.

"Yeah," he replied, extending a hand towards me. "I remember."

His grip was firm and warm, his fingers calloused from years of hard labor. I tried to ignore the way my own hand trembled slightly as we shook hands, or how our eyes seemed to lock onto each other's like magnets.

"Nice to see you again," I managed to choke out eventually, hating myself for sounding so fucking awkward and pathetic.

But if he noticed, he didn't say anything about it. Instead, he just nodded at me once before releasing my hand and turning back towards the logs in front of him.

"Well," Amelia said after a moment, breaking the tense silence that had fallen between us. "I'm gonna go inside and get some water. You two can... chat or something." She raised an eyebrow at me, that playful smirk still on her lips.

Why was she doing this?

Before I could say anything else—before I could even begin to process what was happening—she spun around and walked away, leaving Colton and me standing there alone together.

Fuck. Fuck, fuck, fuck.

I didn't know whether to run after Amelia or make a break for it myself, but before I could decide one way or another, Colton spoke up again.

"So," he said, his voice low and gruff as he picked up the ax once more. "Amelia tells me you're in college."

I blinked at him, caught off guard. Of all the things I thought he might say to me, that wasn't even on the list. "Y-yeah," I stammered after a moment. "Yeah, I am."

He nodded slowly, his eyes never leaving mine as he chopped another log in half. "What are you studying?"

I cleared my throat, trying to find some semblance of composure amidst this whirlwind of anxiety and desire. "Um... art history," I answered after taking too long to do so.

One dark eyebrow rose slightly at that, but he didn't say anything else about it. Instead, he just kept chopping wood, his muscles flexing and bunching with each swing of the ax.

I couldn't help but watch him, entranced despite myself. He moved like someone who knew exactly what they were doing—and did it well—every motion confident and precise.

It was... hot.

No, not hot. Scorching. Like watching some kind of ancient

god at work, each movement mirroring his strength.

I swallowed hard, forcing myself to look away before I got too caught up in the fantasy again. But even then, all I could think about was how much I wanted to run my hands over those muscles, feel them flexing beneath my fingers as he...

"Hey."

Colton's voice cut through my thoughts like a knife, snapping me back to reality so fast that I almost stumbled.

"Yeah?" I asked, trying to sound nonchalant even though my heart was pounding in my chest again. It wasn't working, obviously.

He stopped chopping wood and leaned against the ax handle, his gaze never leaving mine. "You okay?"

I blinked at him, taken aback. That wasn't what I expected him to say—not even close—and for a moment, I couldn't find any words to respond with.

CHAPTER 3

"I'm fine," I said quickly, turning my attention back towards Amelia's house. Anything to avoid looking at Colton any longer than necessary. "Just... It's just so hot right now, you know?"

He raised an eyebrow but didn't say anything else about it. Instead, he leaned against the handle of his ax and crossed his arms over his chest. I tried not to stare at how that made his biceps bulge, or how the movement shifted the muscles in his forearms.

"So," he said after a moment, breaking the silence between us. "You're into art history?"

I blinked, taken aback. It was an innocuous enough question, but coming from him, it felt almost... intimate somehow. Like he actually cared about my answer instead of just making small talk to be polite.

"Yeah," I replied softly, finding myself wanting to tell him more. "It's... It's always fascinated me, I guess. The way people express themselves through different mediums and time periods..."

I trailed off, realizing that I was rambling like an idiot again. But Colton didn't seem bothered—or maybe he just wasn't listening—but instead of making fun of me as most guys would have, he actually nodded.

"Sounds interesting," he said after a moment. "I've always been more of a... hands-on kind of guy myself." He held up his calloused hands for emphasis, and I couldn't help but notice how they looked even larger against the backdrop of his tanned skin.

Damn.

I swallowed hard, trying to ignore the way my body responded to that simple gesture. It was stupid, really. I shouldn't be getting worked up over something so trivial, but I couldn't stop myself from imagining what those hands would feel like on me.

"Right," I managed to choke out, turning my attention back towards Amelia's house again. Anything to avoid staring at him any longer than necessary. "Makes sense."

We lapsed into silence once more, and I could feel the tension building between us with each passing second. It was like standing too close to a bonfire, the heat radiating off of him making my skin flush and my heart pound in my chest.

But then, just as suddenly as it had started, Colton spoke again, and this time, his question caught me completely off guard.

"So," he said, sounding almost casual. "Have you ever worn makeup?"

I froze, feeling like all the air had been sucked out of my lungs. Had he really just asked me that?

"W-what?" I stammered, unable to hide the shock in my voice.

He shrugged one broad shoulder, his gaze like it was eating me whole. "You heard me," he said simply. "Have you ever worn makeup?"

I felt my face grow hot instantly, and I knew I must be tomato-red at this point. How could he possibly know about that? Had Amelia told him?

No, no way. She wouldn't do something like that without telling me first... or would she?

"I... um..." I stammered, searching desperately for some kind of response but coming up empty.

He raised an eyebrow at my hesitation, waiting patiently for my answer. And then it hit me: he was testing me, trying to see if I would be honest with him or not. Maybe Amelia had told him about my little 'secret' after all, and now he wanted proof that I wasn't some big fraud.

Fine. If that's what he wanted, then I'd give it to him.

"Yeah," I answered, forcing myself to look him in the eye as I spoke. "I have worn makeup before."

His expression didn't change, but something flickered in his gaze, something I couldn't quite put my finger on. Satisfaction? Relief?

"You're not afraid of being judged?" he asked after a moment.

I shook my head slowly, finding myself unable to look away from him despite how much it made my heart race. "No," I replied softly. "I don't care what people think anymore."

But that wasn't entirely true. I did care what people thought about me, especially him.

Something shifted in his eyes, and suddenly, the air between us seemed even more charged than before. He took a step closer to me, close enough that I could feel the heat of his body radiating against mine.

"Good," he murmured, his voice low and gruff. "Because there's nothing wrong with expressing yourself however you want to."

I couldn't help but notice how close our faces were now. We were so close that if either of us moved even slightly, our lips would be pressed together.

And of course, I wanted him to do it so bad. To kiss me, to claim me right here in front of God and everyone else...

But instead of doing what I so desperately wished he would, Colton stepped back abruptly, breaking the moment between us.

"So," he said, turning towards the house suddenly. "Did Amelia tell you about her new lipstick?"

I blinked, thrown off guard once again. What the hell was he talking about now?

The word escaped as barely more than a breath—"No"—while I scrambled to piece together thoughts that had scattered like leaves in a storm. My pulse hammered against the silence. "She said nothing about it."

He nodded, turning back towards me with that same unreadable expression on his face. "Yeah, she got this really dark shade, almost black, and it looks fucking amazing on her."

I felt my stomach twist at the way he talked about Amelia's lips, remembering all too well how they had looked when she was wearing that exact color just yesterday...

And then it hit me: why he was talking about makeup like this. He wasn't trying to make small talk or anything; no, he was doing something far more calculating than that.

He was testing me again, to see if I'd react differently to hearing about Amelia's new lipstick compared to his question earlier about whether I'd ever worn makeup myself.

Oh God.

I couldn't help but wonder what else he knew, and how much Amelia had shared with him.

"Well," he said, picking up the ax and starting to chop wood once more. "What do you think about trying some of it yourself sometime?"

I froze, feeling like all the blood had drained from my face. Had he really just...?

"W-what?" I stammered, unable to hide the shock in my voice.

He glanced up at me, his expression almost innocent, if not for that glint in his eyes that seemed to see right through me. "I mean, you said earlier that there's nothing wrong with expressing yourself however you want to," he pointed out with a shrug. "So why not give it a try?"

My mouth opened and closed several times as I struggled to find some kind of response—anything at all—to what he was saying. Was there even anything that could be said?

But before I could manage even a single word, Amelia's voice rang out from inside the house, calling for both of us to do something I didn't understand.

CHAPTER 4

I couldn't believe what I was hearing. Did he really just...? No, there was no way I misheard him. He'd actually suggested that I try on Amelia's lipstick. What the fuck? I never thought he'd say something like that. It was unlike him, to say the least.

My mouth opened and closed like a fish out of water as I struggled to find some kind of response, anything at all, to what he was saying.

"You know," he said casually, leaning against his ax handle once more. "You've got this... look about you."

I blinked, confused and off-balance from the sudden change in topic. "What do you mean?"

He shrugged, his eyes scanning me up and down in a way that made my skin tingle with awareness. "You're just... different. Effeminate, almost."

Effeminate? I certainly didn't think he was going to say that. Some people would say that about me, but him, all of a sudden, bringing that up? It was certainly unexpected.

My face burned, both with embarrassment and something else I couldn't quite put my finger on. Was he... was he making fun of me? Or worse, did he know about the times Amelia had caught me wearing her makeup?

"Excuse me?" I said, my voice harsher than I intended.

He held up his hands, a smirk playing at the corner of his mouth. "Hey, no need to get defensive. I'm not saying it's a bad thing or anything."

I crossed my arms over my chest, trying to hide how much he was affecting me with just his words alone. "Then what are you saying?"

He paused for a moment, considering me thoughtfully before continuing. "You'd look good in a dress, that's all."

My jaw dropped, shock coursing through me. He couldn't be serious, or could he?

"W-what?" I stammered, unable to form any coherent response.

Colton chuckled, shaking his head as though amused at my reaction. "Don't tell me you've never thought about it before."

I felt the blood drain from my face, leaving me feeling cold and exposed. Had he somehow found out about the times I'd dressed up in Amelia's clothes? But no, that couldn't be possible. She would've told me if she had said something to him...

Wouldn't she?

"No," I lied, my voice steady despite how much my heart was pounding. "Never."

He raised an eyebrow at me, clearly not buying it. But before he could press further, I blurted out the first thing that came to mind in an attempt to change the subject and pretend nothing unusual was happening.

"Is this some kind of... joke to you?" I demanded, heat flaring back into my cheeks. "Because if it is—"

"No, of course not," he interrupted, his expression turning serious for once. "It's not a joke. I'm just... being honest."

I studied his face, for a moment thinking more about it than the rest of his body, searching for any sign that he was being anything but genuine. But all I found were those piercing eyes that seemed to see right through me and the hard set of his jaw.

"What about it makes you think that?" I asked, unable to stop myself from taking the bait despite my better judgment.

He shrugged again, turning back towards the woodpile as he answered. "Just a vibe you give off," he answered. "Like you'd be more comfortable in something flowy and soft than... this." He waved a hand up and down my body dismissively, indicating my jeans and t-shirt.

I bristled at that, but before I could say anything else, Colton turned back towards me with another smirk tugging at the corners of his mouth. "Besides," he added. "You've got great skin. Would look amazing with some foundation on it."

I felt my cheeks grow hot again, and this time, there was no hiding the blush that crept up my neck. No one had ever complimented me like that before—not even Amelia when she caught me wearing her makeup.

And coming from him... it meant something different.

"I'm not sure what you think you're doing, but stop it," I muttered, looking away in an attempt to hide just how much he was getting to me with these absurd comments. "You're making fun of me."

He laughed the kind of sound that seemed to rumble through his chest and into mine. "No, really. You've got that kind of face, the kind that can pull off both masculine and feminine features at the same time."

I glanced back up at him, unable to help myself despite how much it made my heart race. "What do you mean?"

He reached out, his fingers brushing against my jawline in a gesture so unexpected that I barely had time to react before he pulled away again.

"Right here," he murmured, tracing the line of my cheekbone with the tip of his finger. "It's high and defined like a model's would be, but then you've got this strong brow and square jaw... It's a good look for you."

I felt my breath hitch in my throat as his hand lingered just long enough to make me wish he'd do it again. God, what was happening right now? Was I actually... enjoying being complimented like this?

Wasn't it what I had always wanted, though?

"And you've got these lips..." He reached out again, his thumb brushing gently over my bottom lip this time.

I couldn't help but gasp at the sudden contact, feeling the heat of him against me like a shockwave through my entire body.

"See?" he whispered, leaning in close enough that I could feel his breath on my face. "You'd look amazing in full makeup and a dress."

I felt my eyes widen as realization dawned on me. He was... seriously considering this. And not just as some passing thought. He actually seemed to be taking it very seriously.

"Wait," I said, suddenly panicked at the idea of him doing something crazy like making me try on Amelia's clothes and makeup right now, in front of him, with him watching everything. "No way. There's no fucking way I'm doing that."

I watched Colton with suspicion, my heart pounding in my chest like a trapped animal trying to escape its cage. "What do you mean, no way?" he asked, an eyebrow quirked up in challenge. "You don't even know what it entails yet."

And all of a sudden, he was being curiously... formal?

I swallowed hard, trying to ignore the way his voice seemed to vibrate through me, making my skin tingle. "Doesn't matter," I said, trying to sound more confident than I felt. "I'm not doing it."

He shrugged, turning back towards the woodpile as though

the conversation was already over. But then, just when I thought he'd given up, his eyes flashed differently.

"You know what?" he continued. "Let's make a deal."

I hesitated, unsure if I even wanted to know what kind of 'deal' he was proposing. But curiosity got the better of me, and before I could stop myself, I found myself asking, "What kind of deal?"

He glanced back at me, his eyes gleaming with something that looked almost like amusement. "I'll show you exactly how I'd turn you into a woman," he started to answer. "And in return, you'll... consider it."

I felt my breath hitch in my throat as the meaning behind his words sank in. Consider it? Was he really giving me an out?

But more importantly, why did that thought both terrify and exhilarate me at the same time?

I kind of knew the answer to that question, though. I just didn't want to think it was real.

"And what if I say no?" I asked, trying to keep my voice steady despite how much my heart was racing.

He smirked, turning back towards the logs in front of him. "Then you'll never know," he answered with a shrug of his shoulders.

I bit my lip, considering his offer. This could be a trap—hell, it probably was—but for some reason, I couldn't bring myself to care. The idea of him describing exactly what he'd do to me... it made me realize how much I wanted it.

"Alright," I said after what felt like years of unnerving silence. "I'm listening."

He chuckled, as though pleased that I'd taken the bait.

"The first thing I'd do," he began, "is shave your face. Close, smooth. No stubble at all."

I felt my stomach twist at the mental image that conjured up. It was intimate, personal... and expectantly hot.

"And then what?" I asked, failing at hiding the need in my voice.

He turned to look at me, his eyes meeting mine for just a moment before he continued. "Then I'd take you shopping."

I blinked, taken aback. Shopping? That seemed... tame compared to what I thought he was going to say.

But Colton just shrugged and kept going.

"New clothes, new shoes, everything," he continued. "We'd find something that makes you feel good when you wear it. Something flowy maybe, or tight and form-fitting..." He trailed off, letting the possibilities hang in the air between us.

I felt my cheeks grow warm at the thought of him picking out clothes for me, trying things on while he waited outside the changing room, imagining how they'd look on my body...

"Next," he said, turning back towards his work. "Hair."

I raised an eyebrow, curious despite myself. "What about it?"

Was there something wrong with it? Because I didn't think so, but maybe there was something he could see that I couldn't.

He glanced over at me again, a smirk playing at the corner of his mouth. "Well, you've got this," he gestured vaguely to my hair, "going on. It's... fine, I guess. But it doesn't do anything for your face."

I bristled at that, not sure what to say or if there was even anything that could be said.

"I'd give you a real haircut," he explained. "Something soft and feminine to frame your face properly." He reached out, his fingers brushing against the strands just above my ear. "Here, maybe."

I felt my breath hitch as his hand lingered there, so close to my face that I could feel the heat radiating off of him.

"And then," he continued, dropping his hand and turning back towards the woodpile once more. He was paying more attention to it than to me, stirring my jealousy. *Fucking woodpile.* I wanted his entire attention focused on me alone in that moment. "Makeup."

My heart skipped a beat at that, memories flooding my mind of the times I'd snuck into Amelia's bathroom and experimented with her lipsticks and eyeshadows. The way it had made me feel—powerful, confident...

But Colton didn't know any of that, and it was best he didn't, because I still wasn't sure if he was trustworthy. As soon as I left, he could start telling people about this conversation.

I didn't even want to imagine that. The mere thought was mortifying—the kind of thing that should be reserved for my worst nightmares and nowhere else.

"I'd start light," he said, his voice thoughtful now as though lost in some distant memory. "Foundation, concealer—just enough to even out your skin tone."

I closed my eyes for a moment, imagining the weightless feeling of him applying makeup to my face, his calloused fingers gently tracing lines and shapes onto my skin...

"And then," he continued without as much as giving me a hint he might stop. "Eyeshadow. Something subtle at first—a neutral shade maybe—but gradually building up to something more dramatic." He paused, turning back towards me again. "You've got great eyes, you know. They'd look amazing with the right colors on them."

I felt myself blush at that, unable to meet his gaze as I mumbled a soft 'thank you.'

He just smiled in response before continuing.

"Lipstick would be last," he said. "Something dark and bold, something that says 'look but don't touch.'"

I swallowed hard, my small dick growing harder with each passing second. The way he talked about it... like he knew exactly what he was doing, like he'd done this before...

But no. That couldn't be right, could it?

I just wanted to know. If the answer was positive, then I had another question: with whom had it happened? Whom had he turned into a woman before meeting me?

"And that's it," he said, wiping the sweat off his forehead. "That's how I'd turn you into a woman."

I stood there for a moment, struggling to process everything he'd just told me. It was so... *thorough*, to say the least. Like he'd actually put thought into this, like maybe he had done it before.

But that couldn't be right...

Could it?

CHAPTER 5

I stood there, stunned and breathless from his detailed explanation, my cock aching in my jeans as I tried desperately to hide my erection from him, not that it was working.

Of course it wasn't working. I was too horny. Always too fucking horny.

That man couldn't know how much he was getting to me, and especially not like this, not when I barely understood what was happening myself.

But then something in his expression changed, a smirk tugging at the corners of his mouth as he took a step closer to me. What was he doing? We were outside. Anybody could see.

"You're hard, aren't you?"

I felt my eyes widen in shock and embarrassment, heat rushing to my face. Of all the things I thought he was to say, that one was definitely not on the list.

"W-what?" I stammered, trying to play dumb despite knowing it was useless. He could see right through me.

Colton chuckled, that dirty smile spreading across his face like wildfire as he took another step towards me, backing me up against the side of Amelia's house until there was nowhere left for me to go.

His hands came up on either side of my head, caging me in, and I felt myself trapped—not just physically, but emotionally too. He had me totally wrapped around his finger.

"Don't lie to me," he murmured. "I can see it. You're like an open book. I can see everything."

And then, I realized something. I wasn't the only one hard in that moment.

My eyes flicked downwards without my consent, and sure enough, there was a noticeable bulge in the front of his jeans.

I couldn't bring myself to ask the question aloud, though. Instead, I just stood there, frozen like a deer caught in headlights as he shortened the distance between our heads, his breath hot against my ear.

"Tell me because I think I know, but still want to be sure," he whispered. "Do you like the idea of me dressing you up?"

My heart pounded in my chest, and I could feel myself getting even harder at his words. This was so fucking wrong, but why did it feel so right?

I opened my mouth to respond—to say something, anything—but no sound came out. It was as though all the air had been sucked from my lungs.

He pulled back by a fraction, just enough to look me in the eye again, and I saw that same gleam of amusement there, along with something else. Something darker, almost twisted…

"You do," he whispered. "Don't you?"

I felt my body betray me then, a shaky breath escaping my lips as I nodded slowly.

God, what was happening to me? Why was I so willing to give in to him like this?

"Say it," he insisted. "I want to hear it from you, or else I won't be satisfied."

I swallowed hard, feeling the weight of his words settle over me like a heavy blanket. But even as my mind screamed at me to push him away, to run as fast and as far from here as possible, I found myself uttering those two tiny words.

"Well, yeah..."

Just as Colton's gaze became more intense, holding mine captive, Amelia's voice rang out behind him.

"Hey, you two," she called out, approaching us with a wide smile on her face. "What are you doing out here?"

Colton stepped back, putting some space between us again, but not before I felt the rough denim of his jeans brushing against mine briefly. I sucked in a sharp breath, trying to regain control over my body and emotions.

Amelia didn't seem to notice anything amiss, though, or if she did, she was choosing not to acknowledge it. Instead, she clapped her hands together, her eyes sparkling.

"I'm so glad you're both still here," she said, looking back and forth between us. "I have something important to show you."

Colton raised an eyebrow at that, turning towards her with a smirk playing on his lips. "Oh yeah? What is it?"

Amelia bit her lip, trying to contain her excitement as she held up a small, rectangular box wrapped in shiny gold paper.

I couldn't help but feel a jolt of embarrassment and betrayal at the realization that Amelia had overheard our conversation, and had possibly even seen how close we were standing to each other just moments before.

But as she looked up at us, her eyes still sparkling, all those feelings were quickly replaced with shock when I saw what she was holding.

"It's a transformation kit," she announced proudly, unwrapping the box to reveal an assortment of makeup and skincare products inside. "I thought we could have some fun trying it out on… someone." Her gaze flicked over to me, and I felt my cheeks flush with heat as I realized what was happening here.

She knew. She fucking knew exactly what we had been talking about, and she was okay with it?

More than okay, even. She looked thrilled at the prospect of turning her best friend into a girl for an afternoon.

"Amelia," I started to protest, my voice coming out weaker than I intended as I tried to find some way out of this. "I don't think—"

But she cut me off before I could finish my sentence, grabbing my hand and pulling me towards the house. "Come on," she insisted, dragging me along despite my attempts at resistance. "You're gonna love this."

Colton followed close behind us, his footsteps steady and confident as we made our way inside. I stole a glance back at him, trying to gauge his expression, but he just gave me a small smirk and shrugged.

Bastard, but I kind of loved it.

"Looks like your best friend has some plans for you," he said, sounding almost… amused?

Amelia led us upstairs to her room, chattering excitedly the entire way about all the things she wanted to do. She talked about how much fun it would be to pick out an outfit for me to wear, and how she couldn't wait to see what I looked like with makeup on.

She didn't even want to discuss her plans, what we were doing, or ask my opinion. Nothing surprising about that, I thought. She'd always been like that.

I listened to her in stunned silence, still struggling to process everything that was happening. This wasn't supposed to happen, and none of this was supposed to be real. It was just a stupid crush, a fantasy…

Wasn't it?

We reached Amelia's room, and she immediately started rummaging through her closet for something "perfect" for me to wear. Colton leaned against the doorframe, watching us with that same amused expression on his face.

"Here," Amelia said after a moment, pulling out a long, flowing dress in a soft shade of pink. She held it up to my body, scrutinizing the fit critically before nodding in approval. "This will look great on you."

I was sure it would, but were we really going to do this?

I stared at the dress Amelia was holding up for me, feeling a sense of disbelief wash over me. This couldn't be real. There was no way this could be happening.

"It's... pink," I pointed out, my voice coming out more sarcastic than I intended. "And it's a dress."

Amelia just shrugged, unfazed. "So?" she said, looking back and forth between me and the dress. "What's wrong with that?"

Colton chuckled from his position against the doorframe, clearly entertained at my discomfort. I would be, too, if I were him.

"Um, nothing," I muttered, shifting uncomfortably under their combined gaze. "I just... this is ridiculous, right? You can't seriously expect me to wear this thing."

Amelia rolled her eyes, but there was still a smile playing at the corners of her mouth. "Why not?" she challenged, holding the dress out towards me like some kind of trophy, and maybe it was... *to her.*

To me, it represented something else, a kind of freedom I thought I'd never have—not openly like this, anyway.

"Because I'm not... that's not something guys do," I said, feeling my face grow hot as I realized how stupid that argument sounded aloud.

But Amelia just laughed and shook her head. "That's exactly the point," she replied, turning towards Colton with a smug smile on her face. "Right?"

Colton pushed off from the doorframe, walking over to stand beside Amelia as he looked me up and down thoughtfully. "You've got the right build for it," he agreed, his voice still filled with that same amusement. "Soft features, narrow hips... We've already talked about this, August."

I felt my mouth drop open in shock at that. Was he really talking about me like this? In front of Amelia, no less?

But then I thought that maybe this shouldn't be so surprising, considering this recent sequence of events. So many things were changing and happening so fast.

"See?" Amelia said, grinning at me. "He thinks you'd look good in it, too."

I stood there for a moment, speechless as they both stared at me expectantly—Amelia with that smug smile still on her face, Colton with his arms crossed over his chest like he was waiting for something.

And then it hit me: they were waiting for me to protest more, to argue against this absurd idea of me dressing up in a woman's clothes.

But... but as much as I wanted to do just that—to put an end to this whole ridiculous charade once and for all—I found myself unable to force the words out.

Because deep down, hidden beneath all the layers of fear and uncertainty and embarrassment, there was a part of me that actually... wanted this. Wanted to know what it would feel like to wear something soft and flowy like that dress—something meant for a woman's body, not mine.

And as if they could sense that hesitation, Amelia and Colton exchanged glances before turning back towards me with matching expressions of triumph on their faces.

"Ah," Colton said, uncrossing his arms and taking a step closer to me. "I think we've finally found the root of the problem here."

Amelia nodded, her eyes wide with excitement and something else. "You're shy about it, aren't you?" she asked, her voice softening slightly as though talking to a scared animal. "That's okay, August. We can take things slow if you want—"

"No!" I blurted out without even fully realizing what it was that I was saying, cutting her off before she could finish that sentence. Because if there was one thing I didn't want right now, it was for them to start treating me like some delicate little flower who needed coddling and protection.

I took a deep breath, steeling myself for what I was about to say next. "I'm not... shy," I managed to choke out eventually, trying my best to sound confident despite how much my heart was pounding in my chest. "I just don't see the point in this whole thing."

Colton raised an eyebrow at that, clearly not buying it. "No?" he said as he took another step closer to me. "Because from where I'm standing, it looks like you've got some pretty strong feelings on the subject."

I felt my face grow hot again, knowing exactly what he was getting at.

"Come on, August," she said, her voice cajoling now as she walked over to stand beside Colton. "You can't keep denying it forever. We know the truth."

I hesitated, torn between wanting to deny everything and just giving in once and for all. But then I saw something flicker in Colton's eyes—something that looked almost... like understanding—and suddenly, I knew what I had to do.

"I'm not a sissy," I said softly, my voice barely more than a whisper as I forced myself to meet their gazes head-on. "I just... I've always been curious about how it would feel, that's all."

There was silence for a moment after that, and I could almost hear the wheels turning in their heads as they processed what I'd just admitted aloud.

And then Colton started to laugh, and it seemed to fill up the entire room. Amelia joined in a moment later, her giggles high-pitched and infectious until both of them were doubled over with laughter, leaving me standing there alone feeling more confused than ever.

"What?" I finally managed to blurt out once they'd calmed down enough for me to speak again. "What's so funny?"

Colton wiped a tear from his eye, still chuckling as he looked back up at me. "You," he said simply. "You're hilarious."

I felt my face grow hot with embarrassment as I realized what was happening here. They weren't laughing at me—they were laughing at how strongly I still refused to admit the truth.

Colton's laughter died down, but his eyes still sparkled with amusement as he looked at me. He still found this whole thing so funny, meanwhile, I was conflicted.

Without warning, he reached out and grabbed my chin between his thumb and forefinger, tilting my head up so I had to meet his gaze.

What the hell was he doing this time? I asked, realizing that also, in that moment, I couldn't ask him that question.

"You're adorable when you're flustered," he said, a smirk playing on the corners of his mouth. "But we both know that's not all there is to it, don't we?"

I felt my breath catch in my throat as I stared up at him, trapped in his hold and unable to move away even if I wanted to—which, admittedly, I didn't.

Being caged in by Colton was a dream come true. I just didn't think that it would happen this way.

"What are you talking about?" I whispered as I tried to keep the tremble out of my voice.

He bridged the gap between our mouths, his lips brushing

against mine briefly before he pulled back again. "You want this," he murmured very slowly. "Admit it."

I felt myself blush at that, knowing exactly what he meant but still unable to bring myself to say the words aloud.

"I... I don't know what you mean," I managed to stammer eventually, looking down and away from him in an attempt to hide just how much his proximity was affecting me.

But Colton wasn't having any of it. He never did. He tightened his grip on my chin, forcing me to look back up at him again.

"You want us to dress you up," he said. Not a question, but an affirmation. "You've always wanted Amelia to pick out an outfit for you and put makeup on your face until you're almost unrecognizable."

I felt my heart pound in my chest at that, knowing all too well just how much truth there was in those words.

"And then," he continued, his lips on the verge of touching mine. "You want me to take it one step further—to shave your face smooth and clean, and maybe even help you try on some of Amelia's clothes too."

I felt myself blush again at that—this time, even hotter than before—and I knew there was no use denying it anymore.

CHAPTER 6

Colton's grip on my chin tightened, his fingers pressing into my skin with a firmness that made me gasp. But it wasn't painful—no, this was something else entirely. It was possessive, commanding, and it sent shivers down my spine.

His eyes burned into mine, intense and unyielding. "You're going to give me what I want," he said, the tone of his voice telling me that he didn't want to argue—not that he needed to, because I wanted to fulfill his wishes.

My heart hammered against my ribs, my mind racing with questions. What did he mean? What could he possibly—?

But before I could even begin to formulate a response, he took a step back, releasing my chin and leaving me feeling suddenly cold without the heat of his hand on my skin.

He unbuckled his belt, the sound of leather sliding through metal echoing in the room like a gunshot. My eyes widened as realization dawned on me—he was going to...? Here? Now?

I opened my mouth to protest, but no words came out. Instead, I found myself watching, hypnotized, as he popped open the button of his jeans and began to lower them down over his hips.

Amelia was beside us in an instant, her eyes wide with

excitement as she took in what was happening right before our eyes. She was just going to watch it happen?

"You're really going to do it?" she breathed, looking up at Colton like he hung the moon. "You're going to let August suck your cock?"

He smirked down at her, never breaking eye contact with me. "Not just let," he replied. "Make."

My stomach twisted, part excitement, part fear. He was doing this to prove something—to make a point about how much power he had over me.

It wasn't really necessary. We both knew that I would do anything for him.

Either way, I couldn't bring myself to care, not when all I could think about was the way my mouth watered at the thought of tasting him.

Colton stepped closer again, his jeans now pooled around his ankles. His cock was already hard, straining against the fabric of his boxers, and I felt a surge of desire so intense it took my breath away.

He reached out, grabbing a handful of my hair and forcing my head back until I was looking up at him. "On your knees," he commanded.

I hesitated for just a moment, some lingering part of me protesting this insane turn of events. Straight guys didn't do stuff like this—not even when they wanted it as badly as I did right now.

But then Amelia was there, her small hands on my shoulders, pushing me down gently until my knees hit the floor with a soft thud. She didn't even have to apply much force. I was already lowering myself anyway.

"Come on, August," she whispered, her voice filled with encouragement and something else—a hint of jealousy maybe?

"Show him what a good little cocksucker you are."

I felt that same thing again—jealousy? From Amelia? But there was no time to dwell on it, not when Colton was already guiding my head towards his cock.

His fingers tightened in my hair as he held me in place, his hips shifting slightly so that the bulge in his boxers pressed against my lips.

"Open up," he ordered.

I obeyed without hesitation, parting my lips and flicking out my tongue to taste him through the thin fabric of his underwear. He groaned, a low sound that sent shivers down my spine, and I felt a sense of power surge through me at the realization that I was doing this to him.

I hesitated for a fraction of a second before obeying, parting my lips wider to take him in. But Colton didn't wait—he grabbed the waistband of his boxers and pulled them down roughly, freeing himself in one swift motion.

My eyes widened as I took in the sight before me. His cock was massive, thicker than anything I'd ever seen, almost inhuman. It jutted out proudly, veins pulsing with blood, a bead of pre-cum glistening at the tip. *Holy shit.* I couldn't believe what my eyes were seeing.

"Jesus," I breathed, my voice barely above a whisper as I stared at it, unable to hide the awe and hunger in my eyes. "You're... you're enormous."

Colton chuckled, his hand still fisted in my hair. "Flattery will get you everywhere with me," he said, guiding me closer until the head of his cock pressed against my lips.

I looked up at him, searching for any sign that this was a joke—that he wouldn't really make me do this. But all I found was that same intense gaze, filled with challenge and desire.

"Open up," he commanded again, pushing forward gently this

time. I complied, letting his thick length slide into my mouth until it hit the back of my throat.

I gagged slightly, tears welling in my eyes as I struggled to take him in. It was too much—too big, too intense—but Colton didn't stop. He held me there for a moment, allowing me time to adjust before pulling back slightly and then thrusting forward again.

"Relax your jaw," he murmured, his voice softening ever so slightly. "Let it slide over your tongue."

I tried to do as he said, focusing on the sensation of him moving in and out of my mouth, filling me completely. He was gentle at first, setting a slow rhythm that allowed me to get used to the size of him.

But then Amelia's voice cut through my thoughts, her words sending a jolt of excitement and jealousy through me. "God, he looks so good like that," she breathed, her eyes wide as she watched Colton fucking my mouth. "His cock is amazing, isn't it, August?"

I moaned around him in response, the vibration making his hips jerk slightly. I didn't want to take my mouth off of it just to answer her question, especially knowing that it was rhetorical.

He groaned, his grip tightening in my hair as he began to pick up speed.

"Fuck, yes," he muttered, his voice strained with effort now. "Take it all, August. Show me what you can do."

My mind raced with thoughts of him and Amelia watching me like this—of how wrong it was, how dirty—but I couldn't bring myself to care. All that mattered was the taste of him on my tongue, the feel of his thick cock sliding in and out of my mouth.

I reached up, wrapping my hand around the base of his shaft, adding pressure as I bobbed my head in time with his movements. He groaned again, louder this time, and I felt a surge of pride at knowing that I was doing this to him.

"Fuck," he panted, his hips moving faster now. "You're going to make me come if you keep doing that." And that was the plan, I thought.

I hummed around him in response, eager to taste him—to swallow every drop—and he let out a low growl of approval. But then, just as I felt his cock swell even more in my mouth, he suddenly pulled back, popping out with a wet, sucking sound.

"Wait," he said, his voice hoarse and breathless. "Not like this."

What?

I looked up at him, confusion warring with desire as I tried to process what was happening. He wanted me to stop? But why?

He took a step back, his cock still hard and glistening with my saliva. "This isn't how it's going to happen," he said, his chest heaving, his skin covered with a thin layer of sweat.

I opened my mouth to protest, but Amelia beat me to it. "What do you mean?" she asked, her brows furrowed as she looked back and forth between us. "Why did you stop?"

Colton glanced at her, a small smirk playing on his lips. "Because I want this to be special," he replied, turning his attention back towards me. "For both of us."

I felt a flutter of excitement in my chest at that—a mix of anticipation and fear as I tried to figure out what exactly he meant.

"But..." Amelia began, only for Colton to cut her off with a sharp look.

"Trust me," he said, his voice brooking no argument. "This is just the appetizer."

I felt my heart pound in my chest at that—at the thought of what was still to come. What could possibly be better than this? Then having him inside me like this?

CHAPTER 7

Colton stepped forward, his large hands wrapping around my upper arms as he led me towards Amelia's en suite bathroom. What was he doing, and what was his plan?

I stumbled slightly, still caught off guard from that blowjob, but he steadied me with an ease that made it clear this wasn't the first time he'd done something like this.

"Where are we going?" I asked, my voice coming out raspier than usual as I tried to hide just how much my body was trembling with anticipation and nerves.

He glanced back at me, a smirk playing on his lips. "We need to get you ready," he replied simply, pushing open the bathroom door and pulling me inside before letting it swing shut behind us.

Amelia followed close behind, her eyes sparkling with excitement as she took in the sight of Colton's hands still resting on my arms. I felt a sudden pang of jealousy at their proximity—at how comfortable they seemed together—but then he was turning towards me again, his gaze intense and unreadable, and all thoughts of anything else faded away.

"We need to get you cleaned up," he said as he released my arms and gestured towards the shower stall. "And shaved."

I felt my face flush at that, at the idea of him seeing me

naked like this, let alone touching me while I was vulnerable and exposed. But there was no use arguing, especially not when every cell in my body seemed to be screaming at me to comply.

Colton turned on the water, letting it run for a moment before testing the temperature with his hand. He didn't seem concerned about his own nudity anymore, standing there casually as though he had all the time in the world, and he most likely had.

I watched him, mesmerized, as he grabbed a towel and placed it on the counter within easy reach of the shower. Then he turned back towards me, his eyes glinting with that same amusement I'd seen earlier.

"You know," he said, walking over to stand directly in front of me. "I've never actually done this before."

My eyebrows shot up at that, confusion warring with disbelief. "What do you mean?" I asked. "Done what?"

He shrugged, a small smile tugging at the corners of his mouth. "Helped someone get ready for their... transformation."

I felt my heart skip a beat at that, at the realization that he was taking this seriously, that he wasn't just messing with me or playing some cruel joke.

"So, you've done the other part before?" I asked, trying to keep my voice steady despite how much it was shaking. "You've helped someone... like this?"

He hesitated for a moment, his eyes flicking away from mine as though lost in thought. Then he nodded slowly. "Yeah," he said softly. "Something like that."

I felt a sudden, overwhelming desire to ask him about it—to know more—but before I could even open my mouth to speak, he was reaching out and grabbing the hem of my shirt.

"Arms up," he commanded, his voice firm as he began to lift it over my head.

I complied without hesitation, lifting my arms above my

head and letting him strip me down until I was standing there in nothing but my boxers. He didn't even seem to notice—his eyes were focused on the task at hand, his movements efficient and practiced.

He knelt down in front of me then, grabbing the waistband of my boxers and tugging them down over my hips. I felt a sudden rush of embarrassment as he exposed me like that, but he didn't seem to care. He just tossed my boxers aside and grabbed my hand, pulling me towards the shower. He didn't even look at my cock.

"In you go," he said, pushing open the glass door and guiding me inside before following close behind.

The hot water was a shock at first, but it quickly turned into something else. It was this slow-building pleasure that spread through me like wildfire as Colton began to lather up the soap in his hands.

He started with my hair, scrubbing it roughly with shampoo until it was sudsy and clean. Then he moved on to my body, using a loofah to wash away all the grime and sweat I'd accumulated over the past few hours.

His touch was firm but gentle, grazing over every inch of me as though he were mapping out each contour and line. He didn't skip any part—my arms, my chest, my back... even the sensitive skin between my legs. He was being thorough.

I gasped at that, when he touched my balls, and he paused for a moment, looking up at me with a smirk on his face.

"Too much?" he asked, raising an eyebrow as though daring me to challenge him. Should I? Probably not.

So either way, I just shook my head, unable to bring myself to voice any protests despite how badly they wanted to be heard. Because the truth was, it felt good and, actually, even better than anything I'd ever experienced before. And I didn't want him to stop. Not now.

He chuckled at that, the sound vibrating through my entire

body as he continued. He washed my legs next, running the loofah over them in long, slow strokes until they were clean and smooth.

Then he stood up, dropping the loofah onto the shower floor with a soft thud. His eyes met mine for just a moment before he reached out, tracing the line of my jaw with his thumb.

"We need to get rid of this," he murmured as he leaned in close enough that I could feel his breath on my skin. It was warm and familiar.

I knew exactly what he meant—the hint of stubble still left on my face.

He grabbed a razor from the edge of the shower stall then, popping open the cap with one hand before bringing it up to my face.

"Ready?" he asked, raising an eyebrow at me as though daring me to say no.

I hesitated for just a moment, just long enough to realize that I was actually doing this, but then I nodded anyway. Because what did I have to lose?

He started with the sides of my face first, working his way up from my jawline to my cheeks in slow, steady strokes. Then he moved on to my mustache and beard, carefully shaving away every last bit until there was nothing left but smooth skin.

I expected to feel a pang of loss but felt nothing at all—just smooth skin where the beard had been—as Colton leaned back again, his eyes scanning me critically as though checking for any missed spots. He didn't miss a single one.

"There," he said, dropping the razor onto the counter behind him. "Now you're clean."

But we weren't done yet, not even close. There was still so much hair to shave.

He grabbed a bottle of shaving cream next, squirting some into his palm before rubbing it between his hands to warm it up.

Then he reached out, pressing his fingers against my chest and spreading the foam over my skin in slow, circular motions.

"Wh-what are you doing?" I asked, my voice coming out breathless. I knew what he was going to do, but still couldn't fully believe it.

He looked up at me, a small smile playing on his lips. "Getting rid of all this, obviously," he replied, gesturing vaguely towards my body hair.

I felt my eyes widen at that, at the realization that he really was going to do this. But before I could even begin to protest, he was already reaching for the razor again.

He started with my chest, even though there wasn't much hair there, running it over my skin in smooth, careful strokes until all that remained were tiny little bubbles of foam and the smoothness of my body underneath.

Then he moved on to my stomach—my abs, my sides... Everywhere but where I really wanted him to go. Not that I was about to say anything, not when his hands felt this good moving over me like this.

He worked his way down to my thighs next, taking extra care around the sensitive skin of my inner legs. And then, finally, he paused—just long enough for me to realize where he was going next.

I felt my breath hitch in my throat as I looked down at him, at the way he was kneeling on the shower floor, his eyes focused intently on his task at hand. He didn't even seem to notice how close his face was to... that part of me. But then again, maybe he did.

Maybe this was all part of some calculated plan to drive me crazy with lust. If so, it was working perfectly.

He reached out, wrapping one hand around my cock and holding it still as he began to shave the hair away from my balls. I gasped at that, and he looked up at me, a smirk playing on his lips.

"Too much?" he asked again, raising an eyebrow as though daring me to say something.

But I just shook my head, unable to force any words past the lump in my throat. Because honestly? It felt good—too fucking good.

He finished with my legs next, running the razor over them in long, slow strokes until they were smooth and hairless. Then he sat back on his heels, his eyes scanning me critically as he checked for any missed spots.

"There," he said, dropping the razor onto the shower floor with a soft thud. "Now you're ready."

But ready for what? To put on makeup first, or the clothes?

I opened my mouth to ask him that very question, but before I could even get a single word out, Amelia was pushing open the shower door and stepping inside.

"Can I help?" she asked, looking back and forth between us with wide eyes. Her gaze flicked downwards briefly, taking in the sight of Colton's naked body, spotting his cock, which was semi-hard now.

Colton glanced up at her, a small smile playing on his lips. "Sure," he said, standing up and gesturing for her to take his place in front of me. "He could use some help with... details."

I felt my face flush at that, at the realization that they were talking about me like I wasn't even there, but then Amelia was reaching out, her fingers grazing over my chest as she began to inspect every inch of my body.

"He looks so smooth," she murmured, running her hands down my arms and back up again. "He looks ready to be transformed."

I felt a shiver run through me at that, at the way she said it, like it was a compliment rather than an insult, and I couldn't help but wonder what that meant for me.

Did I really want to look like a woman? To feel like one, too?

The answer was obvious, even if I didn't fully want to admit it. I let things get to this point because, indeed, I wanted to become a sissy. My entire body yearned to be feminized.

CHAPTER 8

I stood there, dripping wet and completely naked, as Amelia and Colton stepped out of the shower to grab towels before returning to help me dry off. They both took their time, their eyes lingering on my body in a way that made me feel more exposed than ever.

Amelia grabbed a towel from the rack and began to dry her hair, but her gaze never left mine. She smirked slightly, as though enjoying the sight of me like this. I was more vulnerable than ever before, naked, and freshly shaved. Colton was no different. He rubbed his towel over his chest absently, his eyes scanning every inch of my body.

"Well," he said, breaking the silence. "Let's get you dressed."

I felt a flicker of excitement at that, followed quickly—and unexpectedly—by a wave of doubt. Was I really ready for this? To have them dress me up in... girl clothes?

Amelia seemed to sense my hesitation because she reached out, placing a comforting hand on my arm. "It's okay," she murmured, her voice soft and reassuring. "You can change your mind at any time."

Although I appreciated the offer of an escape route, I nodded, knowing I would never take it. There was no way I was backing down from this.

Colton chuckled, tossing his towel onto the counter. "But you won't," he stated, as though he could see right through me. Maybe he could.

He turned towards Amelia then, gesturing for her to grab something from the transformation kit we'd left on the bathroom vanity earlier. She did so without hesitation, returning with a delicate silk dress in a soft shade of pink that shimmered under the harsh fluorescent lighting.

I'd seen it before, of course, but its beauty still surprised me.

"It's... so beautiful," I breathed, unable to tear my eyes away from it.

Amelia smiled at me, holding it up against her own body for a moment before turning back towards Colton. "What do you think?" she asked him, seeking his approval as though this was somehow his decision too.

He raised an eyebrow, looking the dress up and down critically before glancing back at me. "It'll look good on him," he replied. "But we should put something underneath it first."

Amelia nodded, grabbing a pair of silky panties next—the kind with lace trim and barely any coverage—and handing them to Colton. I never thought I would, one day, wear panties in front of Colton.

He stepped closer then, his warm fingers grazing against my hips as he held the panties out for me to step into. I hesitated for just a moment before doing as he asked, feeling a rush of embarrassment as he helped pull them up over my ass.

"God," Amelia breathed from behind us, her voice filled with excitement and appreciation as she took in the sight of me like this. "You look so good in pink."

My cheeks flushed at how openly they were both admiring me now, as though I were some sort of object to be scrutinized and appreciated rather than a person with thoughts and feelings.

Colton smirked again, reaching out to adjust the waistband of the panties slightly. His fingers brushed against my cock in the process, and I felt it stir to life. He noticed, of course—how could he not? But all he did was chuckle softly before stepping back to give me some space.

"Alright," he said, turning towards Amelia again. "The dress next."

She nodded, holding it up for me to slip my arms through the sleeves. I complied without hesitation, feeling the cool silk slide over my skin like liquid satin. It was soft and flowy, falling down to just above my knees.

Colton stepped closer once more, his hands reaching up to the straps of the dress. He adjusted them carefully, his fingers grazing against my collarbones as he made sure everything was in place.

"Perfect," Amelia breathed from behind us. "You look like a princess."

I felt a rush of pride at that, followed quickly—and unexpectedly—by a wave of self-consciousness. Was I really supposed to feel this way? To want this?

Colton must have noticed my internal struggle because he approached me to speak into my ear. "It's okay," he murmured. "You're allowed to like it."

I felt a shiver run through me at that—at the warmth of his breath on my skin and the reassurance in his voice. Maybe he was right. Maybe I was allowed to enjoy this—to want it, even.

Amelia stepped forward, her hands reaching up to grasp the top of the dress. She tugged it down slightly, exposing more of my cleavage—such as it was—and making me gasp at the sudden cool air against my skin.

"There," she said, stepping back to admire her handiwork. "That's much better."

I looked down at myself then, taking in the sight of the dress clinging to my body. It was beautiful, more so than anything I'd ever worn before, but there was something else too, something that made me feel different somehow.

"Wait," Colton said, reaching out to grab my hand and pull me towards him. "There's one more thing."

I raised an eyebrow at that, curious as he reached into the pocket of his discarded pants and pulled out a small, delicate necklace. It was made up of tiny pink diamonds strung together on a thin gold chain, exactly like the ones Amelia had shown us earlier in the transformation kit.

He stepped closer then, his warm fingers brushing against my skin as he began to fasten it around my neck. I felt a flutter of excitement at that, the gentle pressure of his touch, and the way his breath grazed against my ear as he leaned in close.

"There," he whispered right behind my neck, stepping back to admire his handiwork. "Now you're ready."

I looked down at myself again, taking in the sight of the necklace resting just above the neckline of the dress. It was perfect—the final touch that made me feel like... a princess.

Amelia clapped her hands together, her eyes wide with excitement and approval as she took in the sight of me like this. "You look amazing," she breathed. "I can't wait to see what you'll look like with makeup on, too."

And just like that, all my earlier doubts and fears seemed to melt away, replaced instead with a sense of anticipation and excitement at the prospect of whatever was still to come.

Because honestly? I couldn't wait either.

Next, I sank onto Amelia's vanity stool, my heart pounding in my chest. The cool leather of the seat pressed against the backs of my thighs, grounding me for the next part of my transformation. Colton and Amelia stood before me, their eyes scanning my face like artists about to create a masterpiece.

Amelia held up a foundation bottle, her fingers tracing the label. "First, we'll even out your skin tone," she said, twisting open the cap and dipping her fingertips into the creamy liquid. She approached me, her touch feather-light as she blended the foundation onto my face, working in circular motions from my forehead down to my jawline.

Her hands were steady, confident. She'd done this a thousand times before. I watched her reflection in the mirror, her eyes focused intently on her task. She was enjoying this, I realized. Enjoying playing with me like this.

Colton leaned against the vanity, his arms crossed over his chest as he observed our interaction. His gaze flicked between Amelia and me, taking in every detail.

I could almost feel the heat of his stare, burning into my skin. It was almost too much.

Next came the concealer, applied with a tiny brush under my eyes to disguise dark circles I didn't even know I had. Amelia hummed softly as she worked, her brow furrowed in concentration.

Every so often, our eyes met in the mirror, and we shared a small smile.

Colton cleared his throat, pushing off from the vanity to stand behind me now. His hands came down on my shoulders, his thumbs pressing into the tight muscles there. I felt myself tense at first—what he was doing was unexpected—but then warmth spread through me as he began to knead away the tension.

"So far, so good, princess," Amelia said, stepping back to reveal her handiwork. She grinned at me, satisfied with the transformation so far.

Colton's hands stilled for a moment before they moved down my arms, his touch growing more intimate. I swallowed hard, trying to ignore the way my body was reacting to him, especially when he reached my hands and laced our fingers together.

"Let's learn about contouring," he murmured into my ear, my breathing pausing for a moment. His breath tickled my neck, making it difficult for me to focus on anything else.

He picked up an eyebrow pencil from the vanity, his thumb brushing against mine as he handed it over. I took it, our fingers lingering briefly before he released his grip. Heat rushed through me at that simple touch, and I could feel him smirking behind me, as though he knew exactly what effect he was having on me.

"Now," Colton said, guiding my hand up to my eyebrow. "Gently draw a line just above your brow, following its natural shape."

My fingers trembled slightly as I tried to mimic his movements, but he didn't seem to mind. In fact, his hands came down over mine, steadying me as we worked together to create the illusion of higher, more defined brows.

I could feel him watching me in the mirror, the way my face changed with each stroke of the pencil. His eyes lingered on my lips, and I found myself biting them softly in response, drawing his gaze even more.

"Good," he murmured, stepping back to admire our handiwork. "Now for your eyes."

Amelia passed him an eyeshadow palette, and he held it out towards me. "Choose a color you like," he instructed.

I scanned the array of shades, my fingers hovering over a soft gold shimmer. I glanced up at Colton in question, and he nodded approvingly.

"Excellent choice," he purred as he took the palette from me. His thumb grazed against mine once more before he turned towards Amelia. "Could you grab the eyeshadow brush?"

She passed it to him without a word, her eyes sparkling with amusement as she watched us, like she knew exactly what was happening between Colton and me. And yeah, there was no denying it. She knew.

Colton began to apply the shadow to my lids, his touch feather-light as he blended the color up towards my brow bone. He was close now, his breath on my cheek, his chest pressed against my back. I could feel his heart beating in time with mine—fast, erratic.

I stole a glance at him in the mirror, our gazes locking briefly before he looked away, focusing back on his task. But not before I saw that hunger in his eyes. It burned with a familiar intensity.

"Next," Amelia said, breaking the moment as she handed Colton an eyeliner pencil. "Define those lashes."

Colton took it from her without a word, his fingers tracing the line of my upper lash before he began to apply the liner. His hand was steady, confident, but I could feel him growing harder against me, and could see the evidence in the mirror.

I swallowed hard, trying to focus on anything but the way his body was pressed against mine. But it was impossible, especially when he was so close.

He finished with my eyes, stepping back once more to look at me. "Now for your lashes," he said, reaching for a tube of mascara.

I felt a flicker of doubt then—would this be too much? Would I look ridiculous with makeup on? But Colton seemed to sense it because he leaned in close again, whispering directly into my ear.

"You're beautiful just as you are," he murmured. "But this will make you... extraordinary."

His words sent a shiver through me, both at their meaning and the way his voice sounded when he said them. I nodded, giving him permission to continue.

He applied the mascara carefully, his fingers brushing against my lashes with each stroke. When he finished, he leaned back again, letting out a low whistle of approval as he took in the transformation.

"Now," Amelia said, passing Colton a lipstick tube. "The pièce de résistance."

I felt a rush of excitement at that, because this... this would make it real. This would turn me into someone I hardly recognized myself—a sissy, a princess, a boy dressed as a girl.

Colton took the lipstick from Amelia, twisting off the cap before holding it up to my mouth. "Open," he commanded softly.

I obeyed without hesitation, parting my lips slightly and feeling the cool metal of the tube against them. He leaned in close then, his breath mingling with mine as he began to trace the color onto my bottom lip first—slowly, carefully.

My heart hammered in my chest as I watched him—watched us too—in the mirror. His eyes were locked on mine, focused intently on what he was doing. But there was something else too—a hunger to finally bend me over and fuck me senseless.

He finished with my lower lip before moving onto the upper one, his touch gentle yet firm. When he finally pulled away, I let out a shaky breath, one I hadn't even realized I'd been holding in.

Colton's eyes lingered on my mouth for a moment before they flicked up to meet mine again. And that was when I saw it, the desire he couldn't hide anymore.

He bridged the gap between us again, his lips pressing against mine in a soft, chaste kiss that still managed to set my body on fire.

I COULDN'T BELIEVE HE JUST KISSED ME.

He pulled back after just a moment, but the damage was done —my heart raced, and my cock throbbed.

"Fuck," he muttered under his breath as he stepped back to put some space between us again.

Amelia laughed, her eyes sparkling with amusement as she looked back and forth between us. "Well," she said, reaching up to adjust the neckline of my dress slightly. "You're all dressed up now, except for one thing."

She reached into a drawer, pulling out a long, blonde wig

that cascaded down in loose curls. She held it up for me to see, a mischievous grin spreading across her face.

"Congratulations, August. You've finally reached the end of your transformation," she said, stepping behind me and placing the wig on my head.

Now... Now I was finally a sissy.

CHAPTER 9

I stood before Amelia's vanity mirror, my heart pounding like a kick drum in my chest. The person staring back at me... I barely recognized them. Gone was August, the scrawny college kid, replaced instead with this vision of feminine beauty. My lips curled up into a smile as I took in every detail.

The makeup was flawless, each stroke precise and purposeful. My eyes looked huge, framed with long, dark lashes that fluttered when I blinked. It was one of the best things about my makeup.

The gold eyeshadow made them sparkle like jewels under the soft light. My brows were fuller, more defined, thanks to the eyebrow pencil Colton had guided my hand with.

I could still remember every detail and second of that moment.

My cheeks were flushed with a healthy glow, courtesy of the blusher Amelia had applied with delicate precision. And my lips... God, my lips. They were painted a soft pink, plump and inviting. I could hardly keep myself from touching them, from tracing their new shape with my fingertips.

The dress was next to fall under my scrutiny. The silk shimmered like liquid candy floss as it draped over my curves —curves that seemed suddenly more pronounced than before. I knew that wasn't true, but it still felt like it was. It was as if the very fabric itself was accentuating what little I had, making me feel womanly in a way I'd never experienced.

And then there was the wig. Long blonde curls cascaded down my back like a waterfall of sunshine, framing my face and giving me an air of angelic grace. I couldn't help but reach up, running my fingers through the silky strands as I marveled at how real it felt.

But perhaps the most startling transformation was... lower. My hand drifted down, tracing the neckline of my dress until it reached the hem. And then, with a deep breath, I lifted the fabric just enough to glimpse what lay beneath.

There it was: a small, round bulb pressing against my asshole. The butt plug. Amelia and Colton had prepared me for this moment, had eased it into place with gentle hands and patient words. Now, hours later, I could still feel it. It was solid, unyielding, stretching me open in ways that both thrilled and terrified me.

I let the dress fall back into place, taking a deep breath as I tried to process everything. This was who I was now, who they had made me. And God help me, but I loved every minute of it.

Just then, I heard the faint click of Amelia's bedroom door opening. Panic surged through me, my heart pounding even harder as I realized they were coming back.

The door creaked open, revealing Amelia standing there, her cheeks flushed with excitement as she took in the sight of me. Behind her, Colton loomed large, his eyes glinting with hunger as they scanned my body.

"Well, well. Look at you," Amelia breathed, stepping into the room and closing the door softly behind them. "You look... amazing."

I blushed at that, feeling a flutter of pride at their approval. But there was something else too—an antsy excitement in my belly, anticipation coiling through me as I waited to see what they would do next.

Colton approached first, his long strides eating up the distance between us. He reached out, tracing a finger along the neckline of my dress, making me shiver at the contact.

"So precious," he murmured. "But it has to come off. I know you don't want to do that, but it's for something special."

I swallowed hard, nodding as I raised my arms above my head, granting him permission to undress me. He didn't need it—he was already reaching for the hem of my dress, tugging it up over my hips before pulling it off completely.

I stood there in nothing but my pair of pink panties and that butt plug still nestled between my cheeks. I could feel its weight, its presence, reminding me and warning me about what was going to happen.

Amelia stepped forward, her fingers tracing the waistband of my panties before snapping them off with a sharp tug. I gasped, the cool air hitting my skin, making me suddenly self-conscious.

But then Colton's hands were on me again, warm and firm as they explored every inch of my body. He paused at the plug, his fingers tracing around it before giving it a gentle tug.

"How does this feel?" he asked.

I bit my lip, trying to find the words. "It's... big," I admitted, blushing. "But I like it. It reminds me of how much you want me."

It also reminded me of how much he approved of my transformation. I wasn't the same person I used to be. Not even my relatives would recognize me now.

He smirked, leaning in close. "Good," he whispered against my ear. "Because your asshole—we are going to make it even wider."

My heart pounded at that—at the thought of them filling me up with their cocks and that strap-on I'd seen Amelia bring with her.

Colton's hands moved down, cupping my ass and giving it

a firm squeeze before slipping a finger between my cheeks. He traced around the plug, pressing gently against it, forcing a gasp out of me.

"Let's get this out of you," he said as he slowly began to pull it from my body. I felt myself stretching, the sensation both intense and strange as it slipped free with a soft pop.

Colton's hands were firm on my hips as he guided me onto Amelia's bed, pushing me back until I was lying down, looking up at them both. My heart pounded in my chest like a drum solo, echoing the throbbing in my cock that pressed against my stomach.

Amelia stood beside Colton, her eyes gleaming with anticipation as she unbuckled her belt and shimmied out of her jeans. She wore nothing underneath—no panties, no bra—and I caught a glimpse of her pussy before she stepped towards me.

Colton was still fully clothed, his shirt stretched taut across his muscular chest. He reached down, grabbing my legs and pulling them apart roughly. His eyes locked onto mine, intense and commanding.

"Don't move," he growled as Amelia climbed onto the bed between my legs. She smirked at him before turning her attention to me, running her hands up my thighs in slow, tantalizing strokes.

"You like that?" she purred, leaning down to kiss my inner thigh, just above my knee. I nodded, my breath catching in my throat as she continued her ascent, each kiss bringing her closer to where I needed her most.

Colton's hand wrapped around my throat, his thumb pressing against my pulse point. "I said don't move," he repeated, his voice a low rumble that vibrated through me. His hand made me freeze, my body tense and eager.

Amelia reached the apex of my thighs, her breath hot on my skin as she nuzzled against my balls, making them tighten in response. She looked up at me, her eyes meeting mine before she took one into her mouth, sucking gently.

I gasped, my hips bucking involuntarily. Colton's grip tightened around my throat, a warning not to disobey again. I had no choice but to will my body not to move, forcing myself to lie there as Amelia worked her way up, taking my cock into her mouth next.

She was slow at first, her tongue tracing the underside of my shaft before she took me deeper, inch after inch until I felt the back of her throat.

She gagged slightly but held firm, her hands grasping my hips and pulling me closer.

Colton's fingers trailed down from my neck, over my chest, stopping to circle one of my nipples. He pinched it hard, sending a jolt of pleasure-pain through me. Amelia moaned around my penis, the vibration making her shudder in response.

She pulled off without giving me a warning, leaving me panting and wanting more. But she had plans of her own—ones that involved that strap-on she'd brought with her. She reached for it now, unrolling it from where it lay on the bed beside us.

Colton watched her, his eyes narrowing as he took in the size of it. "That's going to be a tight fit," he murmured, reaching down to palm my ass, giving it a firm squeeze.

Amelia couldn't help but laugh, slipping the harness over her hips and buckling it. "He can take it," she said, confidence oozing from every pore as she slicked the strap-on with lube.

I watched them, my heart hammering in my chest as they prepared for what was about to come. My asshole could only clench involuntarily at the thought of taking that massive thing inside me, and Colton noticed.

He grinned wickedly, his fingers still playing with my nipple. "You want this, don't you?" he asked. I nodded, my mouth too dry to speak.

Of course I wanted it. I wanted everything they were going to give me.

Amelia climbed back onto the bed, straddling my hips as she lined up the head of the strap-on with my hole. She looked down at me, her eyes soft for just a moment before they hardened again.

"You're going to take this like a good little sissy," she commanded, pressing forward slowly but steadily until I felt the tip slip inside.

The pain forced a gasp out of me, my body tensing as I tried to accommodate the intrusion. It was too big—too much—but Amelia didn't stop. There was nothing and no one capable of stopping her in that moment, I realized with fear.

She pushed deeper, her hips rolling in a steady rhythm that had me stretching to take every inch, and even with all my effort, it still felt like a losing battle.

Colton watched us, his hand stroking his cock slowly as he took in our joined forms. When did he remove his clothes? I couldn't remember seeing him doing it.

He reached out all of a sudden, grabbing my chin and turning my face towards him.

"Watch," he growled, his eyes locking onto mine as Amelia began to fuck me in earnest now, her hips slamming against me with each thrust. I did as he said, watching as that massive strap-on disappeared inside me again and again.

Even if he hadn't said anything, I would still be watching that thing.

I could feel every ridge, every vein as it moved within me. It was too much, too intense, and yet, I never wanted it to stop. My cock leaked pre-cum onto my stomach, reflecting just how turned on I was despite the overwhelming sensations coursing through me.

Colton leaned down, his lips crashing against mine in a kiss I never thought would happen. I thought he wasn't the kind of man who would kiss, but there he was, proving me wrong.

He tasted of desire and dominance, and I found myself kissing him back with equal fervor, my hands reaching up to tangle in his hair as our tongues danced together.

He pulled back just as suddenly, leaving me gasping for air and with a clear layer of sweat on my body. "Your turn," he said, nodding towards my cock.

I knew what he meant, what he wanted. I sat up, my body still trembling from Amelia's fucking, and turned to face him. His cock stood proud and erect before me.

I reached out while wondering if I should be doing that or not, wrapping my fingers around the base of his shaft. It was hot and throbbing in my hand. I looked up at him in that moment, seeking confirmation that this was what he wanted—and found it in his intense gaze.

"Suck," he commanded as he guided my head towards his cock.

I opened my mouth, taking him inside until I felt the tip hit the back of my throat. He was huge—bigger even than Amelia's strap-on—but I was determined to take every inch if that was what they wanted from me.

I couldn't disappoint them. Most of all, I wouldn't. Disappointing them would mean I failed, and I didn't want to believe I let something like that happen—not now, not ever.

I relaxed my jaw in that moment knowing that I might not get a second chance, breathing through my nose as I began to move, sliding up and down his length in slow, steady strokes. Colton's fingers threaded through my hair, guiding me as he set the pace.

Not having left her spot, Amelia watched us, her hips moving in time with mine as she continued to fuck me while I pleasured Colton. The sensation of being filled both ways was overwhelming, but I loved every minute of it.

I'd always wondered what it would feel like, and I was so happy to be finding out in that moment.

I continued to take Colton into my mouth, feeling him grow harder with each passing second. Amelia's movements became more urgent, her hips slamming against me. The sound of our bodies meeting echoed around the room, mingling with our ragged breaths and the wet, sucking noises coming from my mouth.

Colton's fingers tightened in my hair again despite the pain he was making me feel, guiding me faster along that slab of meat. He was close—I could tell—and that knowledge sent a thrill coursing through me. I wanted to taste his cum for the first time, to feel him pulse on my tongue, and it was the only thing I was thinking about in that moment.

"Hmm, definitely not yet. I don't want to end it like that," he grunted, pulling me off him just as the first spurt of Amelia's orgasm hit her. She cried out, her fingers digging into my hips as she rode out her climax. She was holding on to me so strongly I was sure it was going to leave marks.

Then, with a final thrust, she pulled herself free from me, leaving me empty and aching for more. I didn't want her to go anywhere in that moment.

Noticing the opening, Colton didn't waste any time. He grabbed my legs, flipping me over onto my hands and knees without so much as a warning. He wasn't one to give out warnings.

I gasped at the abrupt movement but quickly adjusted to the new position, eager for whatever he had in mind. It could only be something good. I was sure of it.

"Stay still," he commanded, his eyes flashing with lust. I nodded, burying my face in the pillows as I waited for him to take over.

I felt the tip of his cock press against my puckered entrance, already slick with Amelia's lube. He pushed forward, stretching me open just like she had, but this time it was different. This time, there was no strap-on between us. It was just Colton and me, flesh on flesh.

It wasn't just different, but better. *So much better.* He was making me feel something she couldn't.

He began to move, his hips rolling in a steady rhythm as he filled me completely with each thrust. I could feel every inch of him, every ridge and vein, as he set a punishing pace that left me breathless and trembling.

I could hardly think or speak in that moment; everything was happening too fast.

Colton's hands grasped my hips, pulling me back against him with each stroke. He was relentless, his body slamming into mine with enough force to make the bed frame creak in protest.

Amelia was probably watching everything with a sense of envy. Still, I was surprised she was okay with it. I didn't think she was going to be.

My own cock hung heavy and ignored between my legs, aching for some attention that wasn't coming anytime soon. But I didn't care. I was too focused on the sensation of Colton inside me, too lost in the pleasure-pain that came with each thrust.

I could feel myself building towards something, some point of no return where nothing would matter but the moment we were in and the people we were with. It was like a rollercoaster, climbing steadily higher and higher until I knew there was no going back down.

Colton's fingers dug into my hips, his grip tightening as he neared his point of no return, which was something I was anxiously waiting for. "Jack off for me, sissy," he growled. "It's almost the right time. You're going to come when I do."

I reached down without hesitation, wrapping my hand around my cock and stroking in time with his movements. There wasn't much space, but I made do with what little we had.

It didn't take long—just a few quick pumps of my fist before the pressure inside me became too much to bear.

I finally came, my orgasm ripping through me like a storm as I spilled onto Amelia's bedsheets below. I hoped she wasn't going to mind that.

Colton followed suit just moments later, burying himself deep inside me with a guttural groan as he filled me with his hot, sticky cum.

We fell together in a tangle of limbs and sweat, our bodies still joined as we rode out the last waves of our orgasms. Amelia lay beside us, her eyes soft as she watched Colton pull out of me slowly, his cock glistening with his seed and my sweat.

"Look at that," he murmured, tracing a finger through the mess on my thighs before bringing it to my mouth. I opened without hesitation, tasting him and myself mingled together in that moment.

There was no way I was going to hesitate when the opportunity came. It was everything I wanted to cap off the moment.

"That's how you know I own your ass now," he growled. "My cum inside you—it's a claiming, August."

I nodded, unable to speak as I swallowed down the mixture he had on his fingers. It was more than just physical for me now. I felt claimed, truly claimed, in a way that went beyond sex.

Amelia reached out, her fingers trailing through the mess on my thighs before she brought them to her own mouth, tasting Colton's cum as well. She hummed, satisfied with the flavor of him mixed with mine.

"You taste good like this," she murmured, looking between us with a wicked grin. "And I'm so sad it's over for now. But there will be many more opportunities in the future."

And of that, I was sure—more sure than I had ever been in my life. I didn't want anything else. All I wanted was to keep being their sissy and get fucked senseless.

Thankfully, my wish was being granted.

EPILOGUE

5 years later...

Years had passed since that first fateful night when I—formerly known as August—became the sissy of Amelia and Colton. Oh, how things had changed, yet somehow stayed the same. I wouldn't have it any other way.

I was now their kept boy, living in a sprawling Victorian house with them, tucked away in a quiet neighborhood where the only noise came from the occasional honking goose flying overhead. It was the embodiment of absolute peace.

The house blended antique furniture with contemporary art, reflecting both Amelia's sophisticated eye and Colton's more casual aesthetic.

Colton had retired from his job, opting instead to become a stay-at-home husband, managing our home and finances with the same fierce dedication he once reserved for cutting logs. He'd taken up cooking as a hobby, and the aroma of his homemade stews often filled the entire house, always making my belly growl.

Amelia, on the other hand, had risen through the ranks at her advertising firm, eventually becoming a creative director. She worked long hours, but the payoff was worth it. She could now afford to indulge in her favorite pastime: shopping.

Our closets were overflowing with designer clothes, shoes, and accessories, many of which she insisted I try on just for fun, which I always did because I was her obedient sissy.

Today, as I lay sprawled on the plush velvet chaise in our sunroom—which I knew wasn't common in houses like ours, but we'd had one built because we couldn't live without it—I couldn't help but feel a sense of contentment wash over me.

The warm afternoon sun streamed in through the floor-to-ceiling windows, casting a golden glow over the room. I was dressed in a frilly pink negligee, my hair cascading down my back in loose curls, just the way Amelia liked it.

I didn't need wigs anymore since I let my hair grow naturally now.

Colton entered the room, his eyes drawn to me. He leaned against the doorframe, his arms crossed over his chest, and smirked. "You look like a little princess," he said.

I smirked back, rolling onto my stomach to give him a better view of my ass. "Why, Colton, is that any way to speak to your kept boy?" I teased, fluttering my eyelashes at him.

He chuckled, pushing off from the doorframe and striding towards me. "You know I don't do soft, sissy," he growled, his hands coming down on my ass, giving it a firm squeeze. "But I'll make an exception for you."

I gasped as his fingers drew the lace trim of my negligee, tracing the curve of my ass before slipping between my legs. I spread them willingly, my body begging him to fuck me. And with some luck, I knew he would do it.

"You're already ready for me," he murmured, his fingers brushing against my asscrack. "Did you start without me?"

I shook my head, biting my lip to stifle a moan as he began to circle my dickie with his thumb. "I was waiting for you," I breathed, my hips moving in time with his hand.

He smirked, pulling his hand away just as I was about to come.

I knew he was going to do that, but I still thought it was a dick move.

"Not yet, sissy. You don't get to be so lucky this time," he said, slapping my ass hard enough to leave a mark. "I want you to wait a little while longer."

I pouted, my body trembling as I watched him walk away. I knew he was going to the bedroom, and I couldn't wait to see what he had planned for me.

A few minutes later, he returned, carrying a leather strap and a bottle of lube. He set them down on the chaise beside me, his eyes locked on me, and he couldn't even blink.

"Roll over," he commanded, and I complied without hesitation. I would never dare disobey him. Not even once.

He leaned down, his hands grasping the hem of my negligee before slowly pulling it up over my head. I lifted my arms, allowing him to undress me completely, leaving me naked and exposed beneath his ravenous gaze.

"God, you're beautiful," he murmured, his fingers tracing the curves of my body. "I never get tired of looking at you."

His words earned him a blush from me, my heart fluttering in my chest. I knew I was lucky to have them, to be loved and cared for the way they cared for me.

Colton reached for the strap, wrapping it around my wrists before securing them to the legs of the chaise. I tugged to try something, finding that I was indeed bound, at his mercy.

That realization made him grin, reaching for the lube next. He coated his fingers liberally before bringing them to my ass, circling my hole before pushing inside.

The invasion forced a gasp out of me, my body tensing as I adjusted to the feel of him inside me. He was gentle in the first few seconds, his fingers moving in and out of me slowly, allowing me to stretch around him.

He was being merciful, which was something he sometimes was with me. It didn't happen very often, though, and I preferred it that way.

With my body relaxing, he grew more insistent, his fingers moving faster, harder, until he was fucking me with them, making me writhe and moan beneath him.

Just when I thought I couldn't take anymore, he pulled his fingers out, leaving me empty. I whimpered, my body trembling. I could almost not feel my legs.

"Master, please," I begged, my eyes locked onto his.

My words made him smirk, and he reached for the strap that bound my wrists. "Please what, sissy?" he asked, unbuckling it and freeing my hands.

I was surprised he was already doing that. I thought it would last longer, but either way, I wasn't going to complain. Whatever he had planned for me, I was certain it was going to be good.

"Please fuck me until I can't feel my legs anymore," I moaned, my hands immediately reaching for his belt, eager to undress him.

He chuckled, helping me as I fumbled with the buckle, my hands shaking. When his cock finally sprang free, I moaned, my hand wrapping around it, stroking it gently.

He could only groan in that moment, his hips bucking forward as he thrust into my hand. I could feel his heart pounding through the pulse of his manhood, somehow matching the rhythm of my own.

He grabbed my hips without warning me first, flipping me onto my hands and knees, positioning himself right behind me. The movement made me grit my teeth, my body tense as I felt the head of his cock press against my puckered hole.

He pushed forward without hesitation, his cock stuffing me

completely, stretching me open in a way that made me cry out. He began to move not even a second later, his hips rolling in a steady rhythm that had me gripping the chaise for support, not that it was helping me much.

I could feel every inch of him inside me, his cock rubbing against that spot that created black dots in my vision. I moaned, my body writhing, my fingers curling into the velvet as I held on for dear life.

Colton's hands came down on my hips, his fingers digging into my flesh as he pounded into me, his breathing ragged and uneven.

I thought it wasn't possible, but I could feel him growing thicker inside me, his cock swelling with his impending release.

"I'm going to come inside you," he growled. "I want you to feel me filling you up."

Was there anything else I could do in that moment other than groan?

A second following that thought, my body convulsed as I came around him, my ass clenching tightly around his cock as I rode out my orgasm.

Colton groaned, moaned, and huffed, his body tensing as he came inside me, his hot cum filling me completely.

Moments later, we collapsed onto the surface beneath us, our bodies glistening with sweat, hearts beating in unison. I felt his load seeping from me, trailing down my thighs and pooling on the floor below.

But neither of us cared about that. It was of little importance.

All that mattered was this moment, this connection, this thing that kept us together no matter what.

In the following aftermath, Colton and I lay entwined on the chaise, our bodies glistening with sweat and cum. The room was filled with the scent of sex and the sounds of our breaths slowly returning to normal when suddenly—

click

The door creaked open, and there she stood, Amelia. My goddess, my queen, her eyes locked onto us as if she'd just stumbled upon a scene straight out of one of her dirty fantasies.

"Well, well," she drawled, barely holding back a series of giggles. "Looks like I missed all the fun."

Colton grinned, reaching over to run his hand through my hair. "We were just getting started, love," he said, looking up at her with that hungry glint in his eyes.

It was true—I wasn't done yet. There were still so many things I wanted to do. My sex drive was nowhere near satisfied.

Amelia sauntered towards us, her hips swaying in that hypnotic way she had. She was still dressed from a business meeting—in a sleek business suit that accentuated every curve of her body—and I couldn't help but lick my lips as I took her in. She was going to give me more than a meal—it was going to be a feast.

"August," she purred, stopping before me and reaching out to stroke my cheek. "You look like you've been a very naughty sissy. I need to do something about that."

I blushed at her words, feeling Colton's cock stir against my thigh. I knew exactly what she wanted from me, and I was more than ready to give it.

"I'm always your loyal and obedient servant, Mistress," I whispered, nuzzling my cheek into the palm of her hand.

She smirked, knowing she had me right where she wanted me. "Prove it then," she commanded, hiking up her skirt to reveal the lacy thong underneath. She hooked her fingers into the waistband and slowly slid it down her legs, revealing her shaved pussy to us.

My mouth watered at the sight, my small dickie hardening as I took in her glistening folds. She was already wet and I couldn't wait to taste her.

No, not just that. I couldn't wait to devour her whole.

Colton's hands on my shoulders urged me forward, and I eagerly complied, leaning in to run my tongue along her slit. She moaned, her fingers threading through my hair as she guided me closer.

"You know what I like," she huffed as I circled her clit with my tongue. "Don't be shy now. You know what happens when you are like that."

And I did. I remembered everything, all the punishments, the bad and good things they made me do. It was always a fulfilling experience, despite the pain.

I hummed in response, feeling the vibrations against her sensitive flesh. Her grip on my hair tightened, and she began to grind against my face, fucking my mouth just like Colton had fucked my ass.

Colton could only watch us, his hand working his cock as he took in what his eyes were seeing. I could feel his eyes on me, and it only served to heighten my own arousal.

Amelia's taste filled my mouth and I lapped at her greedily, wanting more of her, all of her. Her moans grew louder, her hips moving faster.

"Don't stop," she commanded, her body tensing as she neared the edge. "Make me come, sissy. Make me fucking come all over your pretty little face."

Hearing that, I redoubled my efforts, flicking my tongue against her clit in rapid succession until I felt her body convulse. She cried out, her fingers pulling at my hair as she rode out her wave of pleasure.

As her tremors subsided, she looked down at me with a wicked grin. "Now," she said, her voice steady despite the climax she'd just experienced. "Lick my pussy clean."

My heart swelled as I lay there, Amelia's scent still lingering on my face. This was it—the life I had always wanted, but thought would never happen. This was real. It was happening now.

Here I was, loved and cherished, desired and dominated, free to explore every fantasy and fetish that had once lurked in the shadows of my mind. My heart fluttered as Colton's fingers trailed along my spine, his touch gentle yet firm.

I turned my head, looking up at Amelia who smiled down at me with warmth and pride.

She was my goddess, my queen, and I wouldn't have it any differently.

This was my life—my perfect, beautiful existence—and nothing would ever change that.

End of Book 5

This series will continue! If you'd like to be notified when Book 6 is released, be sure to click "Follow" on my Amazon page! Don't forget to leave a review—it means the world and makes a big difference.

Here's where you can find the previous stories:

1. My Neighbor Turned Me into the Perfect Woman
2. My Girlfriend Turned Me into the Perfect Woman
3. My Wife Turned Me into the Perfect Woman
4. My Fiancée Turned Me into the Perfect Woman

You can also turn the page to explore my other stories!

MORE BY LUMIA

1. Mighty Good with His Hands: Age Gap Instalove Curvy Girl Novelette
2. Wicked Ride: Curvy Girl, Age Gap, Secret Baby, Mountain Man Novelette
3. He's the Better Man: Cuckold Hotwife Story

ABOUT THE AUTHOR

Lumia spends most of her days imagining the filthiest scenarios possible. When she's in the right mood, she only takes a break when she's done. Her books are always infused with the rawest needs her characters can ever crave.

When she isn't writing – something that doesn't happen often – she's exploring new recipes in her kitchen.

www.ingramcontent.com/pod-product-compliance
Lightning Source LLC
LaVergne TN
LVHW010450150126
829912LV00009B/637